Johnny Lion's Bad Day

Johnny Lion's Bad Day

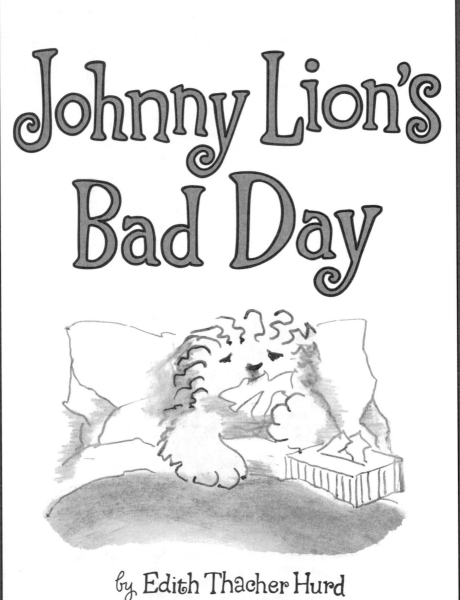

by Edith Thacher Hurd
Pictures by Clement Hurd

SCHOLASTIC INC.
New York Toronto London Auckland Sydney
Mexico City New Delhi Hong Kong Buenos Aires

ISBN 0-439-36745-X

Published by Scholastic Inc., 555 Broadway, New York, NY 10012,
by arrangement with HarperCollins Publishers.
SCHOLASTIC and associated logos are trademarks and/or
registered trademarks of Scholastic Inc.

12 11 10 9 8   7 8 9 10/0

Printed in the U.S.A.   23

First Scholastic printing, December 2001

This book is dedicated to our newest friend:

OBADIAH BUTTERWORTH

Johnny Lion had a bad, bad cold.

Kerchew!

Kerchew!

Kerchew!

Johnny Lion sneezed

and sneezed

and SNEEZED!

"You will stay in bed

all day long," said Mother Lion.

"Oh no," said Johnny Lion.

"Oh yes," said Mother Lion.

9

"Now I will give you your medicine."

"Oh no," said Johnny Lion.

"Oh yes," said Mother Lion.

Then Mother Lion

gave Johnny Lion

some red medicine.

11

"Don't give me any more
of that red medicine,"
said Johnny Lion.

"Not now," said Mother Lion.

"Now go to sleep.

I am going to sweep the house."

Mother Lion began to sweep.

Sweep–sweep–sweep.

13

Johnny Lion did not like

to stay in bed all day long,

so he put his head under the covers.

He closed his eyes.

"Oh–oh–oh," said Johnny Lion.

"I–wish–I–did–not–have–to–stay–in—"

Then he heard a noise.

Swoosh–swoosh–swoosh.

"Whoo–whoo," said something.

"Whoo–oo," it said.

"Whoo–oo is that?" said Johnny Lion.

"It is me," said something.

Johnny saw a big owl.

The owl had big eyes.

The eyes went round and round.

The owl had big wings.

The wings went

swoosh–swoosh–swoosh.

The big owl went,

"Whoo–whoo–whoo."

"Go away," said Johnny Lion,

"or you will catch a bad, bad cold."

"Owls do not catch colds,"

the big owl said.

"Go away anyway," said Johnny Lion.

But the big owl

with the big eyes

that went round and round

did not go away.

It flew here.

It flew there.

It flew closer

and closer and closer

to Johnny Lion, all alone in bed.

Johnny Lion did not know what to do.

19

He could not get out of bed

because Mother Lion had said,

"You will stay in bed

all day long."

20

But just then Johnny Lion went

Kerchew!

Kerchew!

Kerchew!

When he stopped,

the owl was gone.

"Why, Johnny Lion," someone said.

It was Mother Lion.

"You went to sleep under the covers."

"Oh," said Johnny Lion.

"Is that what happened?"

Then Mother Lion gave Johnny Lion

some more of the red medicine.

"It's so bad.

Don't give me any more,"

said Johnny Lion.

"Not now," said Mother Lion.

"Now go to sleep.

I am going to cook supper

for Father Lion."

25

Mother Lion went downstairs

and began to cook something

delicious.

Johnny Lion was so hungry.

He did not want to smell

something delicious,

so he covered up his head.

He closed his eyes.

"I–wish–I–did–not—"

Johnny Lion said.

27

Then he heard someone say,

"Yum, yum, yum.

A delicious little lion."

It was a rabbit,

a big red rabbit,

cooking something

in a big black pot.

29

The rabbit looked at Johnny Lion.

"Yum, yum, yum," the rabbit said.

"Just what I need
for my big black pot."

He began to walk on tiptoe.

"Go away," said Johnny Lion.

"I will give you a bad, bad cold."

"Rabbits do not catch colds,"

the rabbit said.

Johnny Lion

shook his little yellow mane.

He waved his little tail.

But the rabbit

kept on going tiptoe–tiptoe–tiptoe.

Closer and closer and closer.

Very close indeed.

Johnny Lion opened his mouth.

He showed his white teeth.

"Roar!"

went little Johnny Lion.

But the rabbit did not stop.

ONE STEP!

TWO STEPS!

THREE STEPS!

Closer and closer and CLOSER!

Very close indeed.

34

Until—

Kerchew!

Kerchew!

Kerchew!

went Johnny Lion.

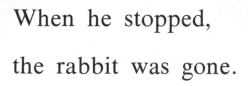

When he stopped,

the rabbit was gone.

36

But a big voice said,

"Where were you?"

It was Father Lion.

"Under the covers," Johnny said.

"Please can't I get out of bed?"

"Not yet," said Father Lion.

"You are still sneezing.

I will give you your medicine."

"Oh no," said Johnny Lion.

"I do not want any more

of that red medicine."

Johnny Lion did not want

any more owls.

He did not want

any more red rabbits.

But Father Lion said,

"Yes, you must take your medicine."

So the little lion

opened his mouth wide

and took the medicine.

Then Father Lion said,
"I will tell you a story.
Once upon a time
there was a little lion
who had a bad cold.
So he put his head under the covers."

"And had bad dreams,"
said Johnny Lion.
"Really?" said Father Lion.
"Really?" said Mother Lion.
She had something delicious
for Johnny Lion's supper.

"Yes, really," Johnny Lion said.

"What did you dream about?"

"Owls and a big red rabbit,"

Johnny Lion said.

42

Then he showed

Mother and Father Lion

how the owl flew.

He showed them

how the big red rabbit went

tiptoe–tiptoe–tiptoe.

44

"Well, well, well," said Father Lion.

"Oh my, oh my, oh my,"

said Mother Lion.

Then they both said,

"What gave you those bad dreams,

Johnny Lion?"

"That bad red medicine," Johnny said.

"Oh, no," said Mother Lion.

"Nonsense," Father said.

Mother Lion sat down

on Johnny Lion's bed.

"I will sing you a song.

Then you will go to sleep

and have sweet dreams

instead of bad."

So Mother Lion sang a song.

"Moon,

Moon,

Yellow

Yellow moon,

Shine on the world,

Keep the world all bright,

And give my little lion

Sweet, sweet dreams tonight."

48

Then Mother Lion put out the light.

Father Lion said, "Good night."

Then they both said,

"You will have

happy, happy dreams tonight."

Johnny Lion did.

As soon as he went to sleep

he had a happy, happy dream.

He dreamed he was not a little lion.

He dreamed he was a big, big lion.

He had a big, big yellow mane.

He dreamed he had big, big paws.

He dreamed he had a big, huge mouth
and big white teeth.

But best of all, he had

a big, huge, enormous

ROAR!

"Roar! Roar! Roar!

Grr-rr-rr roar!"

went the big, huge, enormous lion.

The big, huge lion

jumped out of bed.

"Roar!

GRR-RRRR,"

went the big, huge lion.

He waved his tail.

He stamped his paws.

Then he ran into

Mother and Father Lion's room.

The big, huge lion

opened his mouth wide and went,

"ROAR!"

"Oh, oh, oh," said Father Lion.

"Help, help, help!" cried Mother Lion.

The big, huge lion waved his tail.

He shook his mane.

He stamped his paws.

He opened his big mouth wide.

He showed his white teeth.

Mother and Father Lion

put their heads under the covers.

"Help, help, help!" they cried.

The big, huge lion opened his mouth.

He began to go

"R—" again.

But just then someone said,

"Why, Johnny Lion,

what are you doing out of bed?"

Johnny Lion woke up.

"Did I scare you?" Johnny Lion said.

"Yes, indeed," said Father Lion.

"I thought you were a big, huge lion."

"I was," said Johnny Lion.

Then he said, "Maybe . . .

maybe I will get into your bed.

Then I won't scare you any more."

"Oh good," said Mother and Father Lion.

So Johnny Lion got into bed

and went to sleep.

He slept and slept

until—

"Good morning," someone said.

It was Mother Lion.

"Did you have sweet dreams?"

Father Lion said.

"Oh yes, indeed," Johnny Lion said.

"Good," said Mother Lion.

"You are all well," said Father Lion.

"May I get out of bed?"

said Johnny Lion.

"Of course,"

said Mother and Father Lion.

So Johnny Lion jumped out of bed.

And when he jumped out of bed,

he went,

"ROAR! ROAR! ROAR!!"